wolf

Cast of Characters

This is the button.

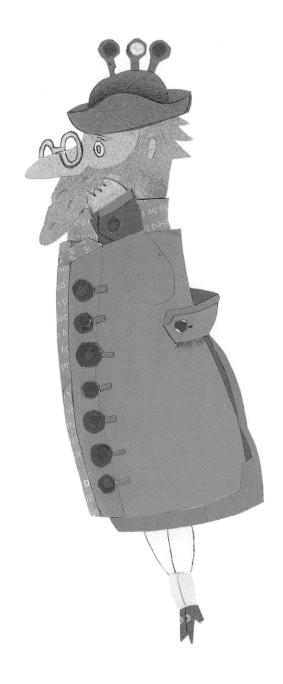

And this is the owner of the button.

This is the little girl...

...and this is the farmer.

This is the wolf...

...and here are the little pigs.
(Not the ones you're thinking of
— these are three *different* pigs.)

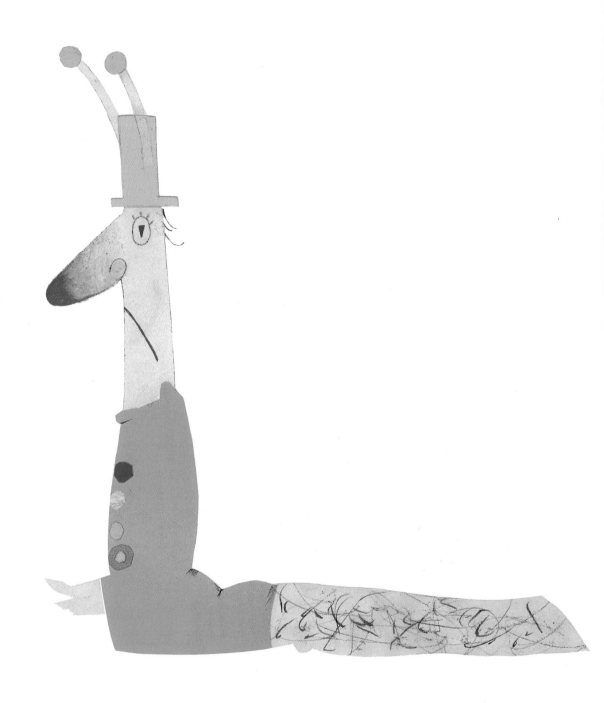

And this is the sad homeless snail.

First North American Edition

First published in Great Britain by ABC,
an imprint of ABC, All Books for Children,
a division of The All Children's Company Ltd.
33 Museum Street, London WC1A 1LD

ISBN 0-316-27393-7

Library of Congress Catalog Card Number 94-6723

10 9 8 7 6 5 4 3 2 1

Published simultaneously in Canada by Little, Brown & Company (Canada) Limited

Printed and bound in Hong Kong

Button

Sara Fanelli

Little, Brown and Company

Boston New York Toronto London

**To my family,
my friends, and
the moon**

The Story

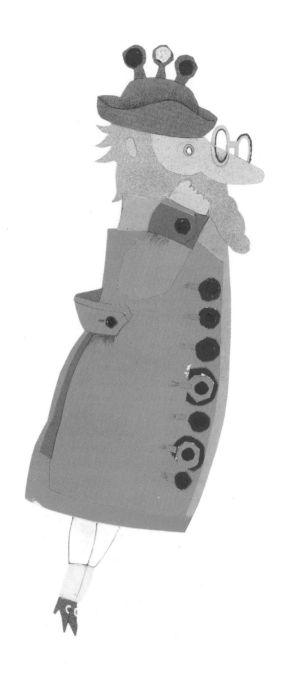

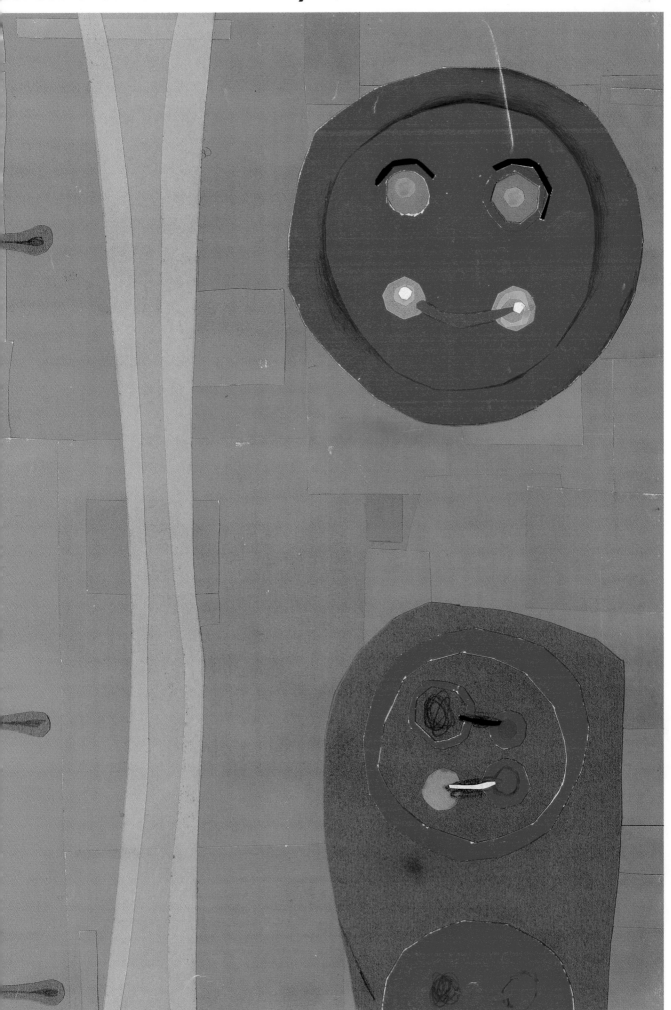

ed buttons that he liked very much. But one button decided to

see the world. He pulled and s t r e t c h e d and pulled and *ping,* he was free.

'til he bounced on the grass. The button's adventures had begun.

The button fell into a pocket, through a hole, and kept falling faster. The button rolled ahead, farther and farther.

Along came the little girl, who saw the button and rolled it along as she ran, faster and

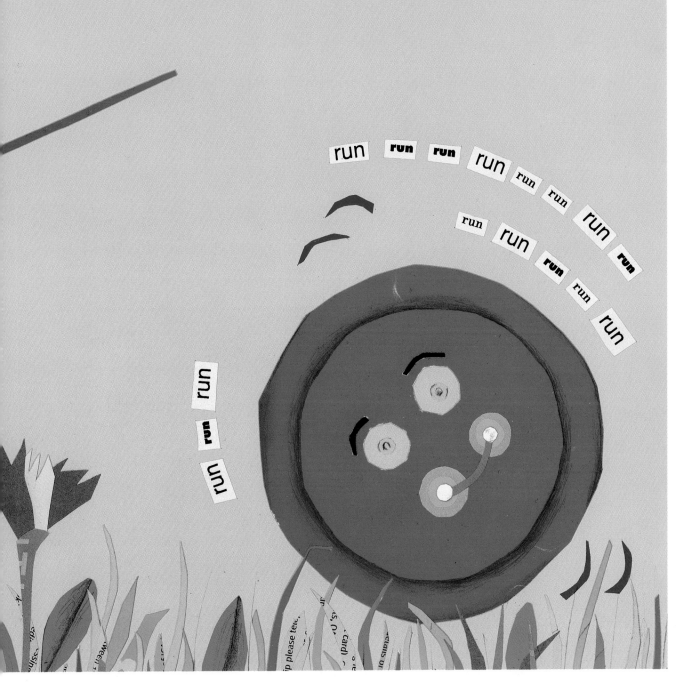

Button ended up in a wide field where a peasant found him

for his cart

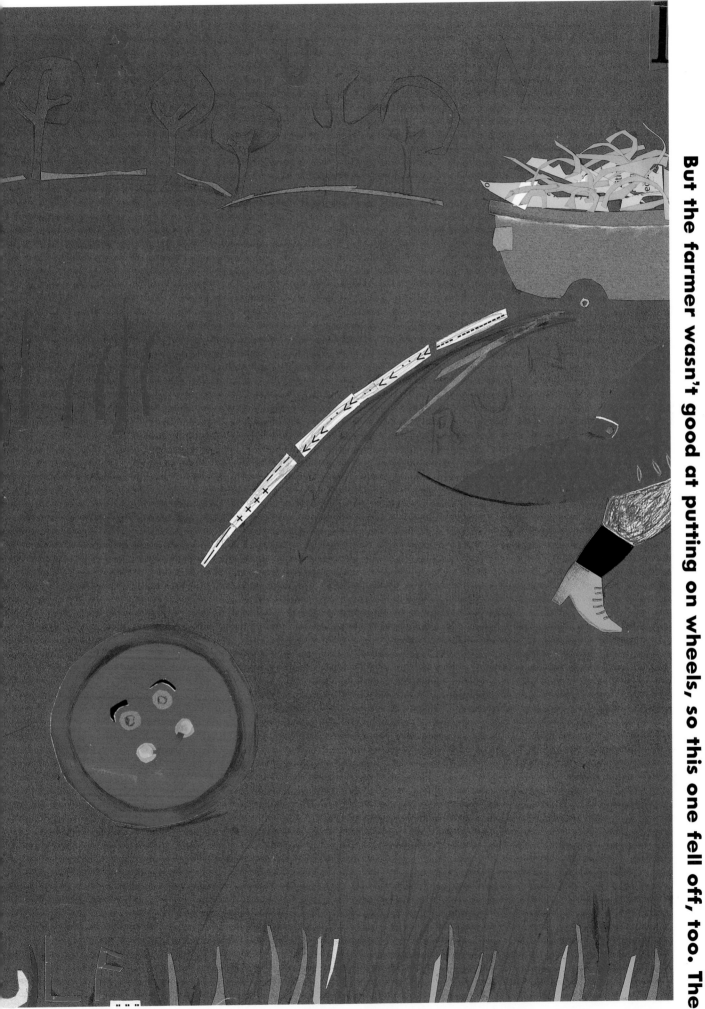

But the farmer wasn't good at putting on wheels, so this one fell off, too. The button rolled right up to a wolf, who knew a good thing when he

the button home with his snout.

pig saw it. "I could use that button," he thought. When the wolf fell asleep, the pig pushed

The wolf took the button home and had a new plate. But a

he ate a good supper and went to bed but

the Pig saw Button through the window and

took away   Butto

his home

It blew the button right off the roof and into a sad homeless snail

e snail adopted the button, and they each had a home.

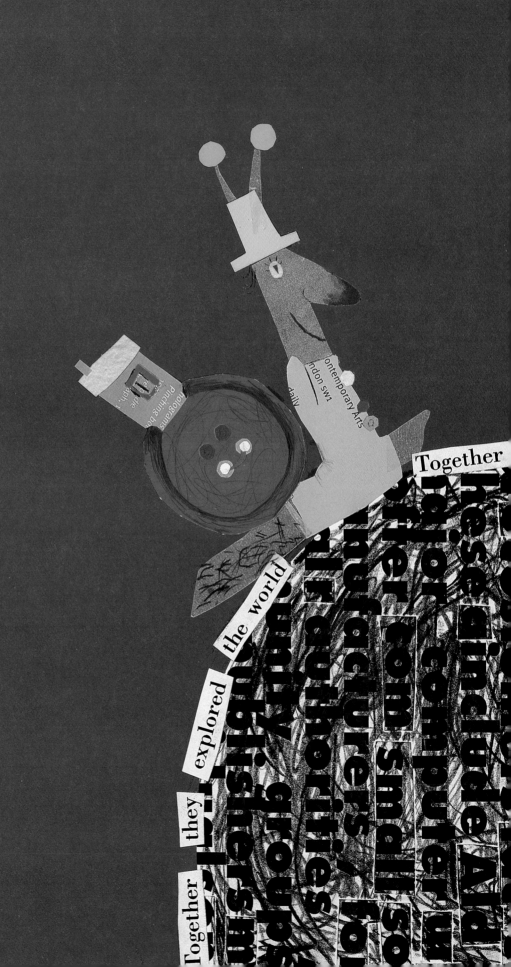

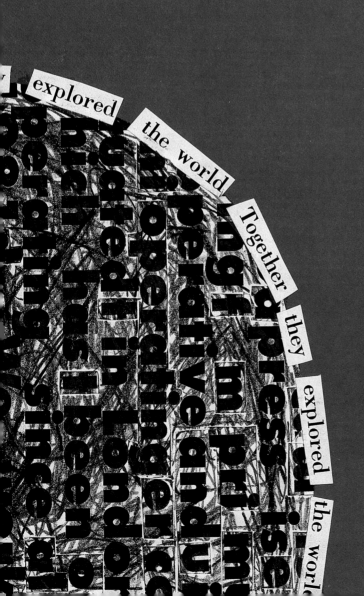

of the button, who had never stopped searching for his beautiful red button, found them.

MY

Until one day the owner

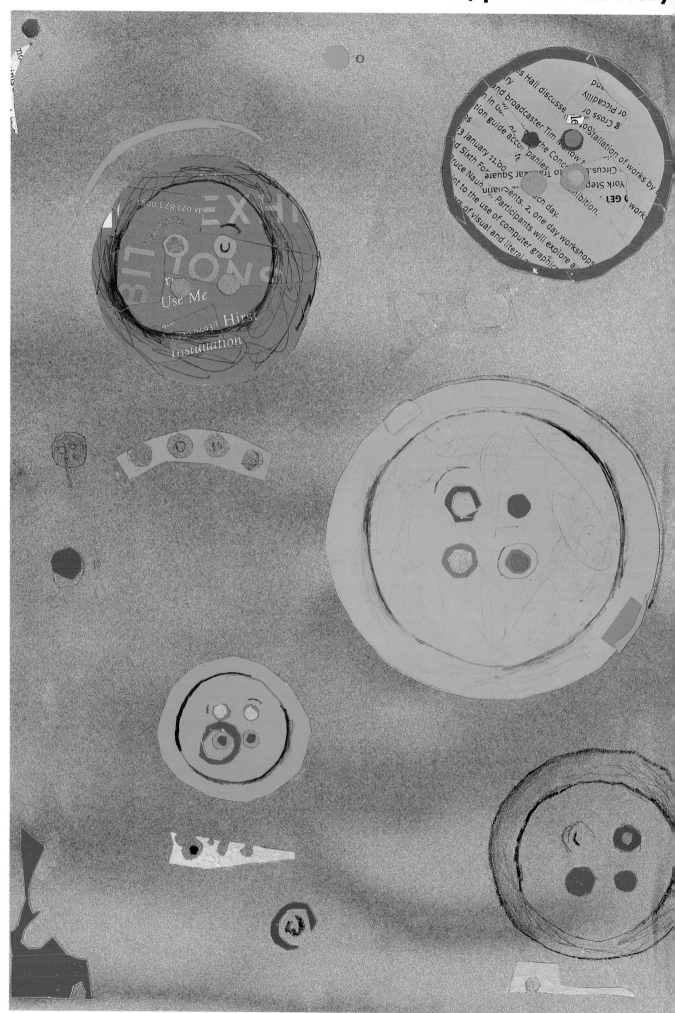

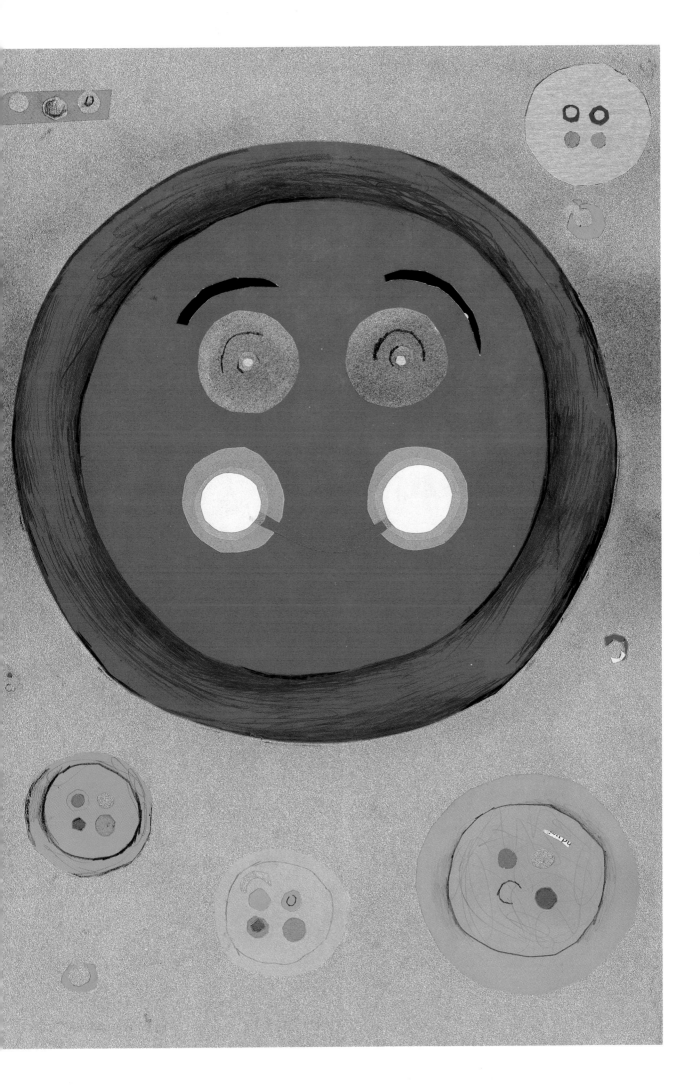

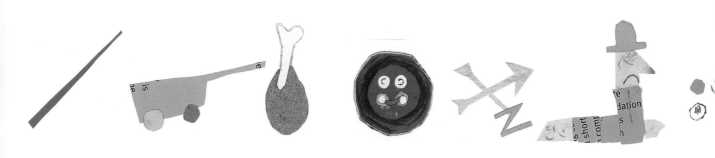

The End